Be a Buddy, Not a Bully

by Michael Scotto

illustrated by The Ink Circle

At the end of a hard day on the farm, Harvest liked to sit by the fire and write in his journal. One evening, Harvest heard a noise outside his window.

It was Buck, the town banker! He was digging away with a shovel at the edge of Harvest's cornfield.

"What are you doing here?" said Harvest.

"Oh, nothing..." replied Buck. "I'm just seeing if my shovel works."

"But why aren't you trying it in your own yard?" asked Harvest. "And why are you dressed like that?"

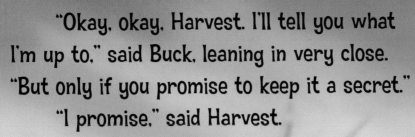

"Okay, okay, Harvest. I'll tell you what
I'm up to," said Buck, leaning in very close.
"But only if you promise to keep it a secret."
    "I promise," said Harvest.
    "I'm digging for treasure!" Buck declared,
and he jammed his shovel in the dirt.

Harvest put his hands on his belly and laughed. "There's no treasure here!" he said.

Buck shook his head and told Harvest, "This map says otherwise."

"I was digging for treasure today down at the river bottom, when I found this map tucked inside a bottle."

"I don't know about any treasure," said Harvest.
"This is just where I plant my ears of corn!"

"Then..." Buck clapped his hands. "I'll just keep
digging and let you know if I find anything."

"It doesn't matter what the map says," Harvest
insisted. "You can't dig here. This is my land. It belongs
to me and my vegetables."

"I'll tell you what," said Buck, raising his eyebrows. "You let me dig on your land...or I'll tell everyone at the market that your vegetables are rotten."

Harvest quickly covered the ears of corn. **"Shh, they'll hear you!"**

Buck squinted his eyes and threw a tantrum,
stomping his feet and **hurling** ears of corn at Harvest.

"Stop that!" cried Harvest.
"Why are you being so mean to me?"
"I wouldn't have to be mean if you'd
let me do what I want!" hollered Buck.
"I don't want to fight," said Harvest.
"I'm going to bed, and I want you to
please go home."
"You're a real spoilsport!"
shouted Buck.

Harvest went inside without a word. The things Buck said to him had made him feel really low. "Dear Journal," wrote Harvest... and when he'd told his journal all about it, he felt a little bit better.

In the morning, Harvest was ready to take some vegetables to the market. But when he got outside, Buck was still digging as if nothing had happened.

"I asked you politely to stop digging on my land," said Harvest. "Now we're going to have a little talk with Chief Tatupu."

"You said you'd keep it all a secret," cried Buck. "You need to stop being such a sourpuss!"

Harvest stood tall. "And you need to stop calling people names. Let's go."

Buck let out a gulp...

...and off they went.

"What can I do for you two?" asked Chief Tatupu, the leader of Midlandia.

"He won't let me dig for treasure!" complained Buck.

"Buck dug holes in my field without even asking," said Harvest. "And he was really mean, hit me with ears of corn, and called me names. I was so upset that I wrote about it in my journal."

Harvest showed Chief Tatupu his journal, in which he had written about how bad Buck had made him feel.

Chief read the journal. "Buck," he said with a sigh, "this is not a good way to make friends. You should be a buddy, not a bully. Harvest, may I show Buck what you wrote?"

Harvest nodded, and Chief handed Buck the journal. "Read this," Chief said, "and then spend a little time by yourself to think about how you have behaved."

Buck went off to read.

When Harvest and Chief were alone, Harvest said, "I feel awful. What did I do to make Buck bully me?"

"When someone bullies you," explained Chief, "it is not your fault. It is the bully's fault."

Soon, Buck returned to Chief and Harvest.
"What do you have to say?" asked Chief.

Buck looked shyly at Harvest. "Harvest, I didn't realize I was hurting your feelings by ordering you around. It was wrong of me to bully you, and **I'm sorry.** Can you forgive me?"

"I forgive you," replied Harvest. "And as long as you don't disturb my vegetables, you can look for your buried treasure."

Buck was amazed. "Really?" he asked.

"Sure!" said Harvest. "When Midlandians are kind to me, I always try to be kind to them."

Harvest led Buck back to the farm and fixed them a dinner of mashed potatoes and corn on the cob. When the meal was done, Buck went back to digging while Harvest wrote about the day in his journal.

And when the moon came out,
they both went happily to sleep.

Discussion Questions

What does it mean to be a bully? Why is it wrong?

What should you do if someone bullies you?